Dawdle Duckling

Toni Buzzeo

illustrated by
Margaret Spengler

DIAL BOOKS FOR YOUNG READERS
New York

For Michael, my first and oldest childhood friend, who spotted Dawdle in the bay and came to tell me so. With thanks for a lifetime of friendship.
—T.B.

To my loving husband, Ken.
—M.S.

Published by Dial Books for Young Readers. A division of Penguin Young Readers Group. 345 Hudson Street, New York, New York 10014. Text copyright © 2003 by Toni Buzzeo. Illustrations copyright © 2003 by Margaret Spengler. All rights reserved. Designed by Kimi Weart. Text set in Bookman. Manufactured in China on acid-free paper • Library of Congress Cataloging-in-Publication Data. Buzzeo, Toni. Dawdle Duckling / Toni Buzzeo ; illustrated by Margaret Spengler. p. cm. Summary: Mama Duck tries to keep Dawdle Duckling together with his siblings, but he wants to dawdle and dream, preen and play, splash and spin. Special Markets ISBN 0-8037-3037-3. 1. Ducks—Juvenile fiction. [1. Ducks—Fiction. 2. Animals—Infancy—Fiction. 3. Mother and child—Fiction.] I. Spengler, Margaret, ill. II. Title. PZ10.3.B963 Daw 2003 [E]—dc21 2001049913.

Special thanks to Holly Roehrich at Delta Waterfowl Foundation and Judy Walker at Maine Audubon Society for their help in explaining mallard duckling feeding behavior.—T.B.

The art was created using pastels.

10 9 8 7 6 5 4 3 2 1

Across the bay
on the blue waves rolling,
one Mama Duck
paddles and quacks.
One, two, three ducklings
swim behind,

but the fourth little duckling
dawdles and dreams.

"Quack! Catch up!"
says Mama Duck.

Dawdle Duckling winds
his zigzag trail.
"NO! Quack! Quack!
I won't catch up."

Up the cove
toward the big rock rising,
one Mama Duck
paddles and quacks.
One, two, three ducklings
swim behind,

but the fourth little duckling
dawdles and dreams,
preens and plays.

"Quack! Catch up!"
says Mama Duck.

Dawdle Duckling nips
his downy fluff.
"NO! Quack! Quack!
I won't catch up."

Along the shore
to the green grass sprouting,
one Mama Duck
paddles and quacks.
One, two, three ducklings
swim behind,

but the fourth little duckling
dawdles and dreams,

preens and plays,
splashes and spins.

"Quack! Catch up!"
says Mama Duck.

Dawdle Duckling splatters
a foamy spray.
"NO! Quack! Quack!
I won't catch up."

Past the marsh
with the cattails waving,

one Mama Duck
paddles and quacks.
One, two, three ducklings
swim behind,

but the fourth little duckling
dawdles and dreams,
preens and plays,

splashes and spins,
dunks and dips.

"Quack! Catch up!"
says Mama Duck.

Dawdle Duckling nibbles
a tasty fly.
"NO! Quack! Quack!
I won't catch up."

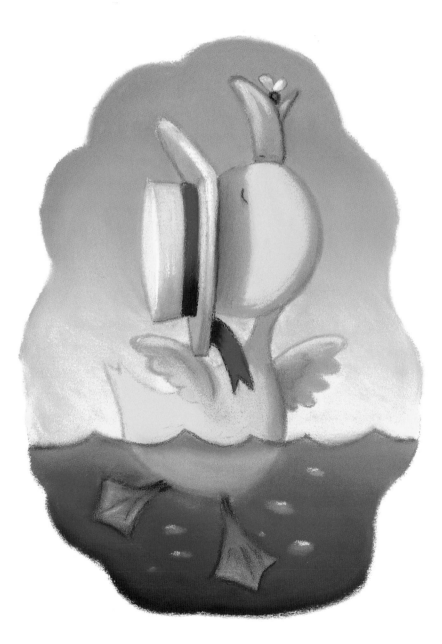

Around the island
in the shallow water waiting—

"*Quaaaaack!*
Look out!"

One Mama Duck
flaps and flutters.

One, two, three ducklings
hop up behind,

but the fourth little duckling
dawdles and dreams,
preens and plays,
splashes and spins,
dunks and dips,
looks—
"*Quack! Quack! Quack!*"

—and **leaps!**
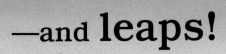

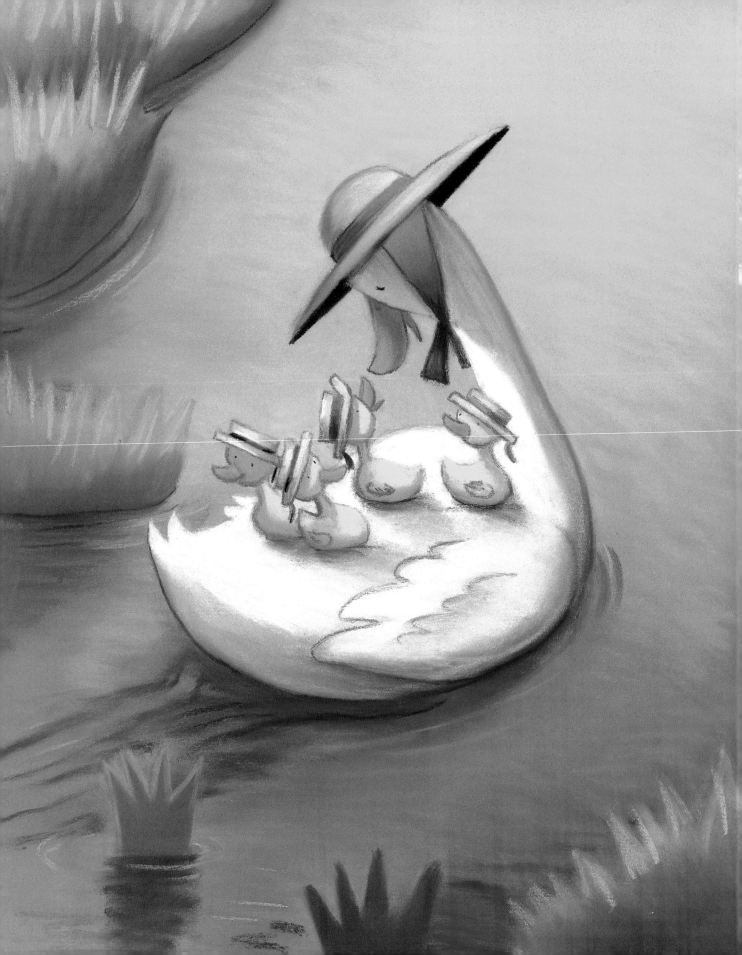